For Woody, Amy, Ben & Rory

All rights reserved. Published in the United States by Dragonfly Books, an imprint of Random House Children's Books,
a division of Penguin Random House LLC, New York. Originally published in hardcover in the United States by Schwartz & Wade Books,
an imprint of Random House Children's Books, a division of Penguin Random House LLC, New York, in 2016.

Dragonfly Books and colophon are registered trademarks of Penguin Random House LLC.

Visit us on the Web! rhcbooks.com

Educators and librarians, for a variety of teaching tools, visit us at RHTeachersLibrarians.com

The Library of Congress has cataloged the hardcover edition of this work as follows:
Zuill, Andrea, author, illustrator.
Wolf camp / Andrea Zuill. —First edition.
pages cm
Summary: "Homer the dog goes away to wolf camp to learn how to bring out his inner wolf" —Provided by publisher.
ISBN 978-0-553-50912-0 (hardback) — ISBN 978-0-553-50913-7 (glb) — ISBN 978-0-553-50914-4 (ebook)
[1. Dogs—Fiction. 2. Wolves—Fiction. 3. Camps—Fiction.] I. Title.
PZ7.1.Z83Wo 2016
[E]—dc23
2015018906

ISBN 978-1-9848-5165-9 (pbk.)

Printed in the United States of America
10 9 8 7 6 5 4 3 2 1
First Dragonfly Books Edition

WOLF CAMP

Andrea Zuill

Dragonfly Books — New York

M_y name is Homer. I am a dog . . .

... but sometimes I am very wolfish.

All dogs have a bit of wolf in them. It's been proven by science.

(This scene may not have actually happened.)

Often I've wondered what it would be
like to live as a real wolf.

Then one day I got a surprise.

WOLF CAMP

HAVE YOU EVER
FELT LIKE HOWLING
AT THE MOON?

COME JOIN US!

WOLF CAMP
Where every dog can
live as a wolf - for
an entire week!

for information call:

1-800-WOLF-CAMP

I *had* to go.

And after a while,

my people thought I should go, too.

Okay! You can go!

The day finally arrived, and I was off!

Then I got to know my fellow campers.

Fang gave us
an important
safety talk.

At last we were ready to be real wolves.

We marked,

howled,

The big moment was here. It was time to hunt!

Before bed I wrote
a letter home.

Dear People,
How are you?
I am fine. The food
here is yucky and has
hair on it. So please
send me some of
Grandma Polly's Pampered
Pooch Doggie Snacks, the
bacon-flavored ones.
Also, send my flea medicine
because there are a lot
of bugs and they are
gross.
Love,
Homer

Smashed
Bug

Ahh-whoooo

Ahh-

Zzzzz

Squeeeeeak!

When it got dark, we found out how real wolves sleep.

I was starting to miss home.

Fortunately, with each day we adjusted to life in the wild.

By the end of camp we were practically wolves.

We were given the certificates to prove it.

Now that it was time to leave, I was feeling
a little sad. (I don't think anyone noticed.)

We howled one last time as a pack.

It was good to be home.

But I had changed. I was no longer plain old Homer. . . .

I was an honorary wolf.